Tennis Club Tension

Story by Diana Noonan

Illustrations by Nathalie Ortega

NELSON
A Cengage Company

Tennis Club Tension

Text: Diana Noonan
Series consultant: Annette Smith
Publishing editor: Simone Calderwood
Editor: Jarrah Moore
Project editor: Annabel Smith
Designer: Kerri Wilson
Series designers: James Lowe and
  Karen Mayo
Illustrations: Nathalie Ortega
Production controller: Erin Dowling
Reprint: Siew Han Ong

PM Guided Reading
Sapphire Level 29

Stranded in Space
Cars: Past, Present and Future
Tennis Club Tension
Second-hand Superstars
Rosamund Zeph: Futuristic Chef
Mapping the World
Working at an Airport
Intrepid Journeys
Sarah's Story
The Amazon Rainforest

Text © 2016 Cengage Learning Australia Pty Limited
Illustrations © 2016 Cengage Learning Australia Pty Limited

ISBN 978 0 17 037936 6

Cengage Learning Australia
Level 7, 80 Dorcas Street
South Melbourne, Victoria Australia 3205
Phone: 1300 790 853

Cengage Learning New Zealand
Unit 4B Rosedale Office Park
331 Rosedale Road, Albany, North Shore NZ 0632
Phone: 0800 449 725

For learning solutions, visit **cengage.com.au**

Printed in Singapore by 1010 Printing Group Limited
6 7 20 19

Contents

Chapter 1   Trouble for the Tennis Club   5

Chapter 2   Mission Impossible   12

Chapter 3   Competition   17

Chapter 4   The Missing Bag   22

Chapter 5   Two Against One   27

Chapter 6   Flat Out   33

Chapter 7   Unwanted Replay   39

Chapter 8   The Apology   45

Chapter 9   Win–Win!   49

Trouble for the Tennis Club

Jake's family was a tennis family. At least, that's what Dad said. Mum said that they were a "community involvement" family, and that tennis was just the way they went about it.

Whoever was right, no one could say Jake's family didn't spend a lot of time at the tennis club. Gramps mowed the grass around the courts. Aunty Diane looked after the coaching roster. Uncle Brent painted the clubhouse. Dad held a fundraising barbecue outside the supermarket every Saturday, and he was also the club treasurer. And as for Mum, she was the club president, and always had been.

"That's just because no one else wants the job!" she always joked, but Jake knew it was because she was so good at her job.

"When people work together, they get along with each other," Dad always said. "And they have fun. You don't have to be a great player to be part of the tennis club! You just have to help keep it running."

Jake felt proud of Dad when he said things like that. Dad could get along with anyone, and he was brilliant at helping everyone else get along, too.

Which was why, when everything began to change in the last week of the school holidays, Jake found himself feeling more miserable than he had ever been in his whole life.

It all started when Mum suddenly hit the brakes as she was about to drive into the club car park, and a platter of fresh salad rolls slid off Jake's knee.

"Oh, what?" Mum wailed.

Jake looked up, clutching the empty platter, to see a shiny black car pulling in front of them.

"Can't that driver read the 'Reserved' sign?" asked Mum.

Mum's parking space was reserved just for her. There was always so much food to carry into the kitchen that she had been given her own parking space close to the buildings.

Mum lowered her window and popped her head out.

"Ah, excuse me," she called to the man who had just stepped out of the black car. "I think you've accidentally parked in the wrong place. That's my space, as I have a lot of food to carry into the clubhouse. Fundraising food."

"The parking here is chaotic!" snapped the man. "If there were half as many parking spaces, but people *paid* to use them, you wouldn't *need* to fundraise!" He leaned back through the window of his car, and Jake heard him say, "Hurry up, Lucas. Get your racquet and get out of the car!"

Mum went red in the face. Then she drove into another parking space that was a lot further away from the clubhouse. She didn't say anything but, as Jake helped her unload the car, he could tell she was upset.

But the man who'd taken their parking space wasn't the worst problem that afternoon. When Jake and Mum approached the clubhouse door, they found a woman with a clipboard and a pen walking around the outside of the building. She was frowning as she jotted down notes.

"Can I help you?" asked Mum.

"Only if you're the president of the club," said the woman, with a professional smile.

"Actually, I am."

"I'm Lisa," said the woman. "I'm from the council. I'm just checking your building for earthquake strength."

Mum frowned. "But we don't have earthquakes in this part of the country."

"Not so far," said the woman, holding up crossed fingers. "But a freak earthquake could happen at any time." She bent over and looked under the clubhouse as if she had lost her tennis ball. "To be honest, I don't like the look of the foundations of this building," she said.

Mum winced. Lisa smiled and tapped the clipboard with her pen. "I'll be in touch in about a week," she said, "once I have the report written up."

"Great," said Mum, when she and Jake were inside. "That's all we need. How are we supposed to find the money to strengthen the clubhouse's foundations, when we only just raised enough to repaint the roof last month?"

Friday afternoons at the club were all about coaching. All the kids got teamed with a senior member of the club, who watched them play and gave them tips. Six times a year, the club hired Ms Drake, a professional coach from out of town, to take groups. The money to pay her came from Mum's salad rolls.

Jake was just putting the rolls into the fridge in the clubhouse kitchen when a loud, angry voice came booming through the wall.

"What do you mean, there's no *professional* coach here this afternoon?" the man demanded.

Mum slid open the hatch that divided the kitchen from the clubhouse lounge, to see what was going on.

"It says on the sign outside that you have coaching here every Friday from 3.30 pm. So where's the coach?"

The man from the shiny black car was standing in the middle of the room. He was waving a pointy finger, almost poking Mr Ansari, the club secretary, in the chest. Mr Ansari was trying to be polite, but Jake could see that he was annoyed.

"We don't have a professional coach here today, Mr Sewell," said Mr Ansari. "But some of our senior players will be coaching, and your son is welcome to join a group. There's no charge."

"Can I?" Lucas asked quietly.

Mr Sewell wasn't listening. "If there was a charge, things around here might be a bit more professional!"

He turned to his son. "Come on, Lucas," he said. "We're going to find a club worth joining."

"He must be new to the area," said Mum, when the man had gone, "or he'd know we're the only tennis club in town!"

Chapter 2
Mission Impossible

Mum told Dad about Mr Sewell but, apart from that, no one thought too much about the scene he'd made at the clubhouse. Everyone was too busy worrying about the council report that was due to come any day.

When it did arrive at the end of the week, the news was as bad as it could have been.

"Replace *all* the clubhouse foundations!" cried Mum, holding the sheaf of papers in her hand. "What's *that* going to cost?"

"Twenty thousand dollars," said Dad, when he came back from calling an engineering friend.

"Twenty thousand!" cried Jake's older sister, Toni. "Mission impossible!"

Jake felt really worried. "It's not the end of the club, is it?" he asked.

"Of course not," said Dad. "Our club is full of people who want to help out. We might be able to do some of the work on the foundations ourselves."

"Our annual meeting is on Tuesday evening," said Mum. "Maybe someone will come along with a smart idea about how to raise the money."

Jake was trying to think of a smart idea of his own when he arrived at school on Monday morning. He was so distracted that it took him a moment to notice Lucas standing in the middle of the classroom, with a group of kids gathered around him. They were looking at a big square watch strapped to his wrist.

"It's a wearable smartphone," Lucas was saying. "It's twice as light as the last model. My dad owns Sewell's Digital, the new electronics shop in town, so I'll be able to get a special discount on these watches for anyone who wants one." He looked up and saw Jake.

"Hi," said Jake.

"Hi," said Lucas, awkwardly.

They had sport later that morning. Mr Peters, the school's physical education teacher, took an equipment box full of tennis balls and racquets out of the storeroom.

"Grab a tennis racquet and pair up!" he told everyone. "Then head over to the tennis courts. Jake, you can be a pair with Lucas. He's new here, so you can demonstrate our routine."

Jake walked over to the volley wall, with Lucas close behind.

"We have ten minutes on the wall, then we play doubles for twenty minutes on the court," Jake said. "You can start."

Lucas threw a ball into the air and served it. He and Jake hit the ball back and forwards against the wall. They were at about the same level of skill, and it was fun taking turns with the shots.

Then Jake was startled to see Lucas's dad walk up and stand on the sidelines. Jake felt Lucas tense up. As soon as Lucas saw his father, he missed the ball.

"You can do better than that!" called Mr Sewell.

Lucas's dad picked up the ball and threw it back to Lucas. "I just thought I'd swing by and see how the first day of school's going," he added.

"I'll bring my own racquet next time," Lucas said to his father. "These school ones are useless."

At lunchtime, Lucas was relaxed and smiling again. He even hung out with Jake and some of his friends. But, as Jake was going out of the gate after school with Lucas right behind him, he spotted Mr Sewell standing by his car.

Lucas seemed to change all over again. "Are you going to the tennis club meeting tomorrow night?" he suddenly asked Jake, loudly enough for his father to hear.

"Yes," said Jake. "Both of my parents will be there. It's the annual meeting to elect committee members."

"I know," said Lucas. "My dad reckons it's time the club got some new leadership."

Chapter 3
Competition

The meeting started as it did every year. Mum and Dad stood up and both said that they would be very happy for someone else to be the president and treasurer.

But instead of the rest of the club members saying, as they usually did, that they hoped Mum and Dad would continue in their jobs, a single voice spoke up.

"Where's the money to strengthen the clubhouse's foundations coming from?" asked Mr Sewell.

"This is the meeting to elect committee members," said Mum. "We'll talk about the funds for the foundation strengthening during the regular monthly meeting."

But Mr Sewell wouldn't listen. He stood up and said loudly that unless the president and treasurer had some ideas about where to find the twenty thousand dollars, they should give up their positions.

There was a surprised murmur from the tennis club members. Before anyone could stop him, Mr Sewell marched up to the front of the room.

"This club needs to change!" he said. "Most importantly, it needs to start charging higher fees, so that it can look after its property."

"We do look after our property," explained Dad. "We do it with voluntary help from our members."

"If we charge too much in club fees," said Mum, "we'll discourage young players from joining, and we won't *have* a club."

Mr Sewell didn't seem to think this was very important. He finished his speech by saying that the Fairgrove Tennis Club needed to join the twenty-first century, and that he was prepared to help them do it if he was voted in as the president.

There was an uncomfortable silence. Then Mr Ansari stood up and said that he thought they should delay the elections until everyone had had a chance to think about how to raise the twenty thousand dollars.

The whole tennis club seemed to be in a huge muddle, and all because of Mr Sewell.

A few days later, something happened at school that pushed Mr Sewell and everything happening at the tennis club out of Jake's mind. Mr Peters made a very important announcement at the end of PE class.

"Gather round," he told the class. "I have got some exciting news. You'll all know that the Smithson Tennis Challenge is being held in the city at the end of the month. And I know you'll all be tuning in to the Sports TV channel to watch Joseph Lord and Diego Fonseca battle it out on the courts. But one lucky person here will get the chance to actually be a part of the games."

"Huh?" asked Jake, feeling a knot of excitement in his stomach. Did Mr Peters have a ticket to give away?

"Each school in the region has been asked to send a twelve-year-old ballboy or girl to help out on the day of the tournament," Mr Peters said.

A ripple of excitement went around the class.

"Our principal has decided that the only fair way to decide who our school will send is to have a tennis tournament of our own," Mr Peters continued. "The overall winner of the tournament will be the ballgirl or boy. The play-offs will take place after school on Wednesday."

Mr Peters smiled at everyone's excitement. "If you want to sign up for the challenge, see me after class."

Chapter 4
The Missing Bag

*T*hat night, at dinner, Jake told his family about the challenge. Everyone was excited for him, but they also seemed distracted and worried.

"Did something else happen?" Jake asked.

"Mr Sewell has emailed everyone in the tennis club asking them to vote him in as the president if they want to save the clubhouse," said Mum. "He says he has a sponsor for the club who'll pay for the foundation strengthening."

"If we rely on a sponsor to do everything for us, we'll lose the community feeling that keeps the club going," said Dad.

"And if we have Mr Sewell as the president, he'll push to increase the club fees," said Mum. "That might mean that lots of families won't be able to afford to play tennis. That isn't the kind of club that we want."

"And I don't want to see a sponsor's advertisements all over our courts," said Toni, jabbing at her dinner with her fork.

Jake agreed, but he couldn't really concentrate on the problem. Instead, his mind was on the play-offs that would happen on Wednesday afternoon.

He knew he was one of the best tennis players in his class, but anything could go wrong on the day. And he really, *really* wanted to be chosen as a ballboy for the tournament.

On Tuesday night, Jake put his tennis gear into his school bag, so that he would be sure not to forget it in the morning. He also packed one of Gran's seed-and-nut bars for an after-school energy boost. Then he went to bed early.

"Good luck," Mum called, as he left for school the next morning.

Jake didn't realise how much luck he would need.

When he arrived at school, the first thing he did was race to the noticeboard outside the office.

He had to check the draw for the tennis challenge. As he looked over the list of names, he felt fairly confident that he would make it into the second and third rounds with no problem. But there was no way of knowing how the final game would go until he knew who he would be competing against.

As the day wore on, Jake's stomach felt so full of butterflies it actually hurt. He thought Lucas might feel the same way, because he asked to go to the bathroom just before the bell rang for home time.

"All the best for the play-offs this afternoon," said their teacher, Ms Lei, as everyone filed out the door.

"Thanks!" said Jake.

But a moment later, he was back in the classroom.

"My tennis gear bag!" Jake said to Ms Lei. "It's gone! Someone's taken it!"

"I'm sure it's there," said Ms Lei, smiling. But when she went out to help Jake look for it in the corridor, she couldn't find it anywhere.

"I have to be at my match in ten minutes," cried Jake, looking at the clock inside the classroom. "I can't play without my shorts and shoes."

Ms Lei began searching in the classroom. Jake walked along the hallway, checking the hooks outside the other classrooms.

When Lucas came back from the bathroom, his tennis clothes on and his racquet in his hand, Jake asked him if he had seen the missing bag. Lucas just shrugged and went outside.

Just when Jake was about to give up, Ms Lei came and found him. "Is this your bag?" she asked.

"It *is*," said Jake. "Where did you find it?"

"A Year 3 student brought it in," said Ms Lei. "She said she found it in the garden."

Jake thought back to Lucas asking to go to the bathroom before the bell. He had a very good idea of how his bag had ended up in the garden.

Chapter 5

Two Against One

The first three rounds of the play-offs were tougher than Jake had expected. But he managed to hold his own and, just as he had hoped, he found himself in the final match.

Unfortunately, his opponent was Lucas. And worse still, Lucas's dad had come to watch.

"You can beat him easily," Jake heard Mr Sewell say, quietly, just as the match was about to begin.

Jake wished Mum and Dad were there to watch the match. He hadn't thought it was the sort of match parents were invited to, though. Now, with Mr Sewell standing on the side of the court, he felt really nervous.

"Good hit, Lucas," said Mr Sewell, each time Lucas returned the ball.

When Jake made a mistake, Mr Sewell said, "That's the way. Keep the pressure on your opponent, Lucas."

As Lucas edged ahead in the points score, Jake thought he would never recover the match. But he kept calm, steadily returning the ball over and over.

At last, he could see Lucas beginning to tire.

"What's wrong with you!" snapped Mr Sewell, after Lucas missed the ball that finally gave Jake the lead.

Lucas bit his lip and didn't look at his dad.

The more Lucas fell behind in the score, the more annoyed Mr Sewell became – and the more mistakes Lucas made.

"Game, set and match!" called Mr Peters at last.

Jake jumped into the air. But he also remembered his manners and went up to the net to shake hands with Lucas.

For a moment, Lucas looked as if he was about to walk off without shaking hands.

"Lucas!" said Mr Peters.

"What?" snapped Lucas, reluctantly putting out his hand.

Lucas shook Jake's hand as quickly as he could, then dropped it.

"You really ought to get these courts seen to," Mr Sewell said to Mr Peters. "The seal's so uneven that it's a hazard."

Mr Peters waited until Lucas and his father had walked towards the car park before he turned to Jake.

"Well done, Jake," said Mr Peters. "You deserved that win." He paused as the doors of the Sewells' shiny black car slammed closed, and added, "Especially as you had two people to play against."

Mum and Dad were nearly as excited as Jake, when he got home with the news that he had been chosen as a ballboy for the tournament.

"How about the clubhouse?" asked Jake, when he'd finished describing the match. "Has anyone thought of a plan to find the twenty thousand dollars?"

Dad shook his head. "No, but we've got until the end of the month to work on it."

"Not if Mr Sewell keeps speaking to the media," said Mum.

"What's happened?" Jake asked.

Mum pointed to the local newspaper lying on the table. "He's told a reporter that the tennis club is run by a bunch of amateurs who don't want to move with the times."

"That's not right," said Toni. She sat up straighter, looking outraged. "Just because we don't want to turn our club into a place where only rich people can play, it doesn't mean we don't know what we're doing."

"Some of the top tennis players started out in small community-run tennis clubs like ours," said Dad. "Diego Fonseca is one of them. I read an article about him the other day, and it said he and his dad used to paint their clubhouse themselves!"

"I can't believe I'll get to meet him when I'm a ballboy at the tournament," said Jake.

The thought of being on the court with one of the country's greatest players made his heart thump. He couldn't wait.

"When do you start the ballboy training?" asked Dad. "The tournament's only a couple of weeks away."

"This weekend," Jake told him. "And the weekend after next is the tournament. It's going to be so cool!"

"It's an amazing opportunity," said Mum. She hesitated. "Although I don't know if you could call it *cool*. They said on the weather report earlier that a heatwave is predicted over the next few weeks. Don't forget to pack your water bottle."

Chapter 6
Flat Out

Mum was right. The weather grew warmer and warmer, and showed no sign of cooling down. When the morning of the tennis tournament finally arrived, the weather report predicted the day's temperature would be higher than ever.

"Make sure you drink plenty of water," said Dad, as he and Mum dropped Jake off on the big day. "You'll be running around a lot, and you need to be careful not to become dehydrated."

Jake got a text message from Toni as he was getting out of the car. She was planning to watch the match on TV, at home.

Don't forget to wave to the camera for me! And tell Diego Fonseca I think he's cute.

No way! Jake texted back, grinning.

Jake was still smiling as he put his phone back into his pocket. He was nervous, but he was happy to think that Toni would be watching. He hoped all his friends at school were going to watch, too.

At the tournament centre, Jake joined the rest of the ballboys and girls. Everyone was talking at once as they passed through the VIP lounge on their way to the courts, but even with all the noise, Jake heard an unmistakable voice. It was Mr Sewell. He was talking to a group of men sitting on big leather sofas by the windows overlooking the tennis courts. Lucas was next to him.

"Fonseca doesn't stand a chance against Lord," Mr Sewell was saying. "He didn't get that professional start to his career that winners need. These amateur clubs don't do anyone any good in the end."

Lucas looked up just as Jake was going past.

"Hi," said Jake. Lucas looked like he was going to answer, but then his father looked up, and Lucas closed his mouth.

When they got to the courts, the woman who'd been training Jake and the others was there to meet them.

"Remember what you're doing today," she said. "The players are depending on you."

"And don't forget to drink plenty of water," added an umpire as he passed. "It's very hot out there today!"

Jake was so nervous as he walked out onto the court that his legs were shaking a little bit. He couldn't imagine what it would be like to be actually *playing* in the tournament.

And as for the heat, it was unbelievable! By the time Diego Fonseca walked onto the court, an hour into play, the digital temperature display read 35° Celsius.

As the balls flew back and forth at lightning speed, Jake focused as hard as he could on doing his job well. It was non-stop action. He was sure he was working as hard as if he had actually been playing the game. But when he carried Fonseca's towel onto the court, and Diego smiled at him and said, "Thanks," it was all worthwhile.

With all the excitement, Jake didn't notice the feeling of nausea that was slowly creeping up on him. By the time he was aware of it, he was feeling really sick, and his head was throbbing. And even though it was so hot, he actually began to shiver.

Water, he thought to himself. *I've forgotten to drink!*

Jake looked around for his water bottle as Joseph Lord prepared to serve, but he couldn't see it.

"Have you seen my water bottle anywhere?" he whispered to the girl he was teamed up with.

"Sorry," she whispered back. "I'll help you look after this set, if you like. Play's starting again."

Jake didn't know what to do. He couldn't leave the court to look for his water bottle, but he wasn't sure if he could carry on the way he was. All he could hope was that the set would be over quickly.

As soon as play started again, Jake had to swoop back and forth, on and off the court, collecting and delivering balls. He had just bounced a ball to Joseph Lord when he suddenly knew without a doubt that he wasn't going to make it. He turned to tell his supervisor he wasn't feeling well. As he did, he felt the ground wobble under his feet.

The next thing he knew, he was lying flat on his back and a first-aid officer was standing over him. Jake felt too awful to even be embarrassed. Still, when he heard the first-aid officer call for a stretcher, he knew he had messed up big time.

Half an hour later, he was on the phone to his mum, asking her to come and pick him up.

"I can't believe I didn't remember to drink," he moaned.

"Think of it as a lesson learned," Mum said. "Never mind. I'm glad that you're feeling better, now."

But that afternoon, lying on the sofa at home, Jake couldn't stop thinking about it.

"I stopped play in the middle of Lord's serve," he said. "Everyone at school is going to be talking about me, and saying how useless I am."

"No one will even know," said Toni. "I was watching TV and *I* didn't see what happened. They filled in the time you were on the ground with some action replay of the game."

She grabbed a sports magazine off the table. "All anyone will be talking about is my hero's amazing final shot," she said, planting a big kiss on the front cover, which displayed a photo of Diego Fonseca. "I just knew he'd beat Lord."

Chapter 7
Unwanted Replay

*T*hat night, as he watched the coverage of the tournament on the news, Jake was relieved to see that his faint wasn't reported at all.

But only a few minutes later, he got a text from an unknown number.

Dad saw the horrified look on Jake's face. "What's the matter?" he asked.

Jake couldn't take his eyes off his phone.

"What are you looking at?" asked Toni. She sat down on the sofa beside Jake and leaned over to look, too.

"Oh, what!" she gasped. "Who's *done* this?"

"Done what?" asked Mum, coming into the lounge.

"Someone has posted a clip online of Jake fainting on the court," said Toni. "It's called 'Ballboy wrecks Lord's chances.'"

"The video has 90 hits, and it was only posted ten minutes ago," said Jake. It was all he could do not to cry.

"Whoever posted it must have sent the link to other people, too," said Toni.

"Who would *do* something like this?" asked Mum.

The landline rang. Dad answered it. He listened for a moment, then Jake heard him say, "Thanks. We've already seen it."

"That was your PE teacher, Mr Peters," said Dad, coming back into the living room. "He was sent a link to the clip, too. He's trying to see if they can have it taken down."

"This is cyberbullying," said Toni angrily. "Who would do such a thing?"

"Lucas and Mr Sewell were at the game," said Jake, slowly. "I saw them on my way to the courts."

"I'm going to go around to the Sewells' house and ask them if they are responsible!" Dad exclaimed. "This unpleasantness has got to stop, before it divides our community as well as the tennis club."

But before Dad could go anywhere, the front doorbell chimed. Toni went to see who it was. Jake heard her open the door, and then heard a choked sound. He looked up to see her standing stock-still in the open doorway.

"C-come in," she finally managed to stutter. She stepped back to let their visitor inside.

Mum and Dad stood up, but Jake felt like he was glued to the sofa, when he saw who it was.

"I hope you don't mind my calling round like this," said Diego Fonseca. He looked at Jake and gave him a smile. "I was just passing by on my way to my hotel, and I wanted to stop in and see how you were feeling. Your supervisor from the match gave me your address."

"Well," said Dad, when it was obvious Jake was speechless, "your visit couldn't have come at a better time. Jake is definitely in need of some cheering up right now, and not just because of his heatstroke."

Diego Fonseca listened carefully as Dad explained about the online clip.

"It's all to do with our tennis club," said Jake, when he'd gotten his voice back. "We were fine until Mr Sewell arrived in town and wanted to change the way we do things."

Mum made a wry face. "Well, not exactly *fine*," she said. "There is the problem of finding twenty thousand dollars before the end of the month."

"Or accepting sponsorship and watching our club turn into something we don't want," said Dad. "You see," he added, warming to his subject, "we're do-it-yourselfers. Some of our members don't even *play* tennis – they just like to help out."

"Sounds like the club I went to when I was a kid," said Diego. "If it wasn't for little clubs run by volunteers, with free coaching, I'd never be where I am today."

He smiled at Jake. "And perhaps you'd never have earned the chance to be a ballboy, without all the practice time and coaching at your club."

"I'm really sorry about what happened today," said Jake. "I should have remembered to drink more water."

"Forget it," said Diego, shaking Jake's hand. "We all make mistakes. I'm glad you're feeling better."

"Could I have your autograph before you go?" asked Toni, holding out a pen and the magazine with Diego's photo on the cover.

"Absolutely," said Diego, with a smile.

He signed the magazine and gave it back to Toni. Then he turned to Mum and Dad.

"Keep up the good work at your club," he said. "It's thanks to people like you that so many kids today can get the chance to play tennis."

Chapter 8

The Apology

Jake wasn't looking forward to school on Monday. When he got there, though, he was surprised to find that almost everyone in his class made a point of saying "Hi" to him. It seemed as though they thought posting the clip had been a mean thing to do, too.

Lucas wasn't in class. Jake thought he must not have come to school, but when the principal, Ms Oliver, called Jake into her office just before morning break, Lucas was already there.

"Lucas has admitted responsibility for posting the clip online," Ms Oliver told Jake. "He says that he is sincerely sorry. This kind of bullying isn't something the school can take lightly, however."

She seemed to be waiting for Jake to give his opinion. Jake wished a hole would open up in the floor of Ms Oliver's office and swallow him. Or that aliens would suddenly appear and whisk him away.

"Cyberbullying is very serious," Ms Oliver said. "It's sometimes even a matter for the police."

Lucas had been looking at the floor. Now his head shot up. His face was white.

Jake thought about Lucas and how, whenever his father wasn't around, he was like any other kid. It was when his dad was there that Lucas became mean.

It's not Lucas who's the bully, Jake thought to himself. *It's his dad. Mr Sewell bullies everyone, including his own son!*

Lucas looked down at his shoes again. "I'm really sorry," he said. It was very quiet, and he didn't meet anyone's eyes, but it sounded like he meant it.

"Lucas will be saying sorry in assembly, as well," Ms Oliver said. She sounded doubtful, and Jake could tell that she was wondering whether that was enough, or if she should punish Lucas with something serious, like a suspension.

"Everyone can make mistakes," said Jake. "I think we should just forget it."

Ms Oliver looked at him carefully, and then at Lucas. "Very well," she said finally. "We *will* give you a second chance, Lucas, but nothing like this must ever happen again."

"It won't!" Lucas said immediately, lifting his head again. "I promise."

That afternoon, Jake went to his friend Cohen's house after school. They had a science project to work on. He had dinner there, and then Cohen's mum dropped Jake off at the tennis club for the new meeting to elect committee members.

He had no idea what had been happening at his place while he was at school.

Chapter 9
Win–Win!

When Jake arrived at the tennis club, the meeting room was packed. Mum and Dad were already sitting up the front.

Jake slid into a seat right behind Mr Sewell and Lucas.

Mum called the meeting to order. Before she could continue, though, Mr Sewell stood up.

"I can't see any point in carrying on until everybody hears my announcement," he said. "We have a major sponsor for the Fairgrove Tennis Club."

There was a murmur from the rest of the room. Jake could see people frowning at the rude way Mr Sewell had interrupted, but there were other people who looked interested.

"The sponsor is my store," Mr Sewell continued. "Sewell's Digital." He held up a cheque. "This is twenty thousand dollars for the foundation strengthening."

Everybody stared, and another murmur broke out. Mr Sewell clapped his hands. "We're going to transform this club into a professional facility that we can all be proud of," he said importantly. "Sewell's Digital Tennis Club is going to be one of the best regional clubs in the country. With professional coaches every weekend!"

"The *Sewell's Digital* Tennis Club!" gasped Jake, as an uncomfortable mutter went around the room. Mr Sewell couldn't be serious!

"Actually, Mr Sewell," Jake heard Mum say, over the babble that was beginning to rise, "your sponsorship isn't required." She smiled. "We already have our funding. And the generous donor doesn't require the club to change its name."

The room fell silent. Everyone's attention snapped back to Mum as she continued.

"I'm pleased to announce that Diego Fonseca agreed to be our club's patron, today! And he's started by making a donation of fifteen thousand dollars."

"That – that's not going to meet the full cost of strengthening the building!" spluttered Mr Sewell.

Now it was Dad's turn to stand up. "Mr Fonseca offered to donate the full cost," he said. "But we discussed it with him, and we agreed that that's not what we need. Like us, Diego Fonseca believes that voluntary work is what makes a club strong."

Some of the other club members were nodding in agreement.

"The remaining five thousand dollars will be found through fundraising," Dad said. "We've talked to the council, and they've given us until the end of the year to have the work done."

People began to clap, and in a moment the applause was thunderous.

Jake saw Mr Sewell turn to Lucas. "Come on!" he said. "We're leaving. These people obviously don't want to do things professionally."

"But, Dad," Lucas pleaded, "there's only one tennis club in town. Where will I play if I don't play here? Please don't walk out. *Please?*"

Jake felt really sorry for Lucas. Mr Sewell really was a bully, and Jake knew he wasn't going to listen to what his son wanted. Jake wished there was something he could say.

Suddenly, Dad started speaking again, from the front of the room.

"We appreciate that you want to improve the club, Mr Sewell," he said. "And even though Fairgrove Tennis Club doesn't need a business sponsor, we *would* be very grateful for help from Sewell's Digital."

Mr Sewell had been on the verge of leaving. Now he sat back down, slowly.

"The club is in great need of a digital scoreboard," Dad continued. "Now that we are fundraising for the foundation strengthening, we won't be able to put any money towards buying one. Is a digital scoreboard something Sewell's Digital would be willing to donate?"

Jake was so proud of Dad. He was giving Mr Sewell a chance to help out in a way that would let him feel important, as well as being good for the club. He was giving him the chance to become a real part of the club.

"Please, Dad?" whispered Lucas. "I want to join the club. I *really* want us both to play for Fairgrove."

There was a long pause as everyone waited.

Mr Sewell licked his lips, nervously. Then he cleared his throat.

"I think my business may be able to install something along those lines," he said.

"And perhaps it could include a digital temperature gauge, as well," added Dad. "So players remember to drink plenty of water when the weather is very warm."

"I'm sure that would be possible," said Mr Sewell.

Everyone burst into a round of applause, including Jake. He didn't know if it was for Dad or for Mr Sewell, but it didn't seem to matter. Everyone was happy. Lucas was looking at his dad with a huge smile.

The meeting continued with the election of officers. Mum and Dad were re-elected as the president and treasurer. To Jake's surprise, Dad then nominated Mr Sewell as a member of the fundraising committee.

"Why did you do *that*?" asked Jake, when the three of them were on their way home.

"Whoever is for you can't be against you," said Dad. He turned around in the passenger's seat, and smiled at Jake. "With Mr Sewell on our side, we won't have any enemies."

"Mm," said Jake, "that's a point." He brightened, an idea occurring to him.

"Maybe I'll ask Lucas if he would like to be my partner in my doubles match on the weekend," Jake said. "That way, his dad won't give me a hard time."

"While you're at it, why don't you ask Lucas if he'd be willing to volunteer to mow the lawns around the courts?" suggested Dad. "It's time someone took over that job from Gramps. You and Lucas could do it together."

"You and your volunteering!" Jake said, laughing.

He knew Dad was right, though. Working together *was* a great way to get along.